To

_____

From

_____

For Holly and the Bowmans, with love   C.J-I. xx

Written and compiled by Julia Stone
Illustrations copyright © 2014 Cally Johnson-Isaacs
This edition copyright © 2014 Lion Hudson

The right of Cally Johnson Isaacs to be identified as the illustrator of this work has been asserted by her in accordance with the Copyright, Designs and Patents Act 1988.

Published by Lion Children's Books
an imprint of
Lion Hudson plc
Wilkinson House, Jordan Hill Road,
Oxford OX2 8DR, England
www.lionhudson.com/lionchildrens

ISBN 978 0 7459 6467 6

First edition 2014

Acknowledgments
"The Owl and the Pussycat" (p20) is by Edward Lear (1812–88).
"Who has seen the wind" (p59) and "Boats sail on the rivers" (p63) are by Christina Rossetti (1830–94).
"O, the grand old Duke of York Had woollen underpants" (p48), "Great oaks from little acorns grow" (p65), and "Climb a silver ladder" (p88) are by Lois Rock, copyright © Lion Hudson.
"Twinkle, twinkle, little star" (p88) is by Jane Taylor (1783–1824).

A catalogue record for this book is available from the British Library

Printed and bound in China, May 2014, LH25

The Lion Book of
NURSERY
RHYMES

Compiled by *Julia Stone*

Illustrated by *Cally Johnson-Isaacs*

LION
CHILDREN'S

CONTENTS

PLAYMATES

GIRLS AND BOYS COME OUT TO PLAY

Girls and boys come out to play
The moon doth shine as bright as day
Leave your supper and leave your sleep
And come to your playfellows in the street.
Come with a whoop, come with a call
Come with a good will or not at all.
Up the ladder and down the wall
A halfpenny roll will serve us all.
You find milk and I'll find flour
And we'll have a pudding in half an hour.

Lucy Locket Lost Her Pocket

Lucy Locket lost her pocket,
Kitty Fisher found it.
There was not a penny in it,
Only ribbon round it.

LITTLE MISS MUFFET

Little Miss Muffet
Sat on a tuffet,
Eating her curds and whey;
There came a great spider
Who sat down beside her
And frightened Miss Muffet away.

JACK AND JILL

Jack and Jill went up the hill
To fetch a pail of water
Jack fell down and broke his crown
And Jill came tumbling after.

Then up Jack got and home did trot
As fast as he could caper
And went to bed to mend his head
With vinegar and brown paper.

When Jill came in how she did grin
To see Jack's paper plaster
Her mother, vexed, did scold her next
For laughing at Jack's disaster.

LITTLE JACK HORNER

Little Jack Horner
Sat in a corner
Eating a Christmas pie.
He put in his thumb
And pulled out a plum,
And said, "What a good boy am I!"

LITTLE BOY BLUE

Little Boy Blue, come blow up your horn,
The sheep's in the meadow,
The cow's in the corn.
Where is the boy who looks after the sheep?
He's under the haystack, fast asleep!

LITTLE BO PEEP

Little Bo Peep has lost her sheep
And doesn't know where to find them.
Leave them alone and they'll come home,
Bringing their tails behind them.

Little Bo Peep fell fast asleep
And dreamt she heard them bleating,
But when she awoke, she found it a joke,
For they were all still fleeting.

Then up she took her little crook,
Determined for to find them.
She found them indeed, but it made her heart bleed,
For they'd left their tails behind them.

It happened one day, as Bo Peep did stray
Into a meadow hard by,
There she espied their tails side by side
All hung on a tree to dry.

She heaved a sigh, and wiped her eye,
And over the hills went rambling
And tried what she could, as a shepherdess should,
To tack again each to its lambkin.

ANIMALS

LADYBIRD, LADYBIRD

Ladybird, ladybird, fly away home,
Your house is on fire, your children are gone –
All except one, and her name is Ann,
And she crept under the frying pan.

OLD MACDONALD HAD A FARM

Old MacDonald had a farm
E I E I O
And on that farm he had a cow
E I E I O
With a moo moo here
And a moo moo there
Here a moo, there a moo
Everywhere a moo moo
Old MacDonald had a farm
E I E I O.

And on that farm he had a sheep…
With a baa baa here…

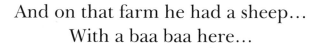

18

And on that farm he had a pig…
With an oink oink here…

And on that farm he had a dog…
With a bow wow here…

And on that farm he had a cat…
With a meow meow here…

And on that farm he had a hen…
With a cluck cluck here…

And on that farm he had a duck…
With a quack quack here…

THE OWL AND THE PUSSYCAT

The Owl and the Pussycat went to sea
In a beautiful pea-green boat,
They took some honey, and plenty of money,
Wrapped up in a five-pound note.

The Owl looked up to the stars above,
And sang to a small guitar:
"O lovely Pussy! O Pussy, my love,
What a beautiful Pussy you are."

Pussy said to the Owl, "You elegant fowl,
How charmingly sweet you sing.
O let us be married, too long we have tarried;
But what shall we do for a ring?"

They sailed away, for a year and a day,
To the land where the Bong-tree grows,
And there in a wood a Piggy-wig stood
With a ring at the end of his nose.

"Dear Pig, are you willing to sell for one shilling your ring?"
Said the Piggy, "I will."
So they took it away and were married next day
By the Turkey who lives on the hill.

They dined on mince, and slices of quince,
Which they ate with a runcible spoon.
And hand in hand, on the edge of the sand
They danced by the light of the moon.

Pussycat, Pussycat

Pussycat, pussycat, where have you been?
I've been up to London to look at the queen.
Pussycat, pussycat, what did you there?
I frightened a little mouse under her chair.

I Love Little Pussy

I love little pussy, her coat is so warm,
And if I don't hurt her she'll do me no harm.
So I'll not pull her tail nor drive her away,
But pussy and I very gently will play.

Three Blind Mice

Three blind mice, three blind mice,
See how they run! See how they run!
They all ran after the farmer's wife
Who cut off their tails with a carving knife
Did ever you see such a thing in your life
As three blind mice?

Hickety, Pickety

Hickety, pickety, my black hen
She lays eggs for gentlemen.
Gentlemen come every day
To see what my black hen doth lay.

I HAD A LITTLE HEN

I had a little hen, the prettiest ever seen.
She washed me the dishes, and kept the house clean.
She went to the mill to fetch me some flour,
And brought it home in less than an hour.
She baked me my bread, she brewed me my ale,
She sat by the fire and told many a fine tale.

A Wise Old Owl

A wise old owl lived in an oak
The more he saw the less he spoke
The less he spoke the more he heard.
Why can't we all be like that wise old bird?

Three Little Owls

There were three little owls in a wood
Who sang hymns whenever they could
What the words were about
One could never make out
But one felt it was doing them good.

INCEY WINCEY SPIDER

Incey Wincey Spider went climbing up the spout
Down came the rain and washed the spider out.
Out came the sun and dried up all the rain
So Incey Wincey Spider went up the spout again.

BAA, BAA, BLACK SHEEP

Baa, baa, black sheep,
Have you any wool?
Yes sir, yes sir,
Three bags full:
One for my master,
And one for my dame,
And one for the little boy
Who lives down the lane.

I Had a Little Pony

I had a little pony
His name was Dapple-Grey
I lent him to a lady
To ride a mile away.
She whipped him and she slashed him
She rode him through the mire
I would not lend my pony now
For all that lady's hire.

When Cows Get Up in the Morning

When cows get up in the morning,
They always say, "Good day,
And how are you this morning,
And is it time to play?"
"MOOO, MOOO,"
That's how they say "Good day".
"MOOO, MOOO,"
That's how they say "Good day".

When sheep get up in the morning,
They always say, "Good day,
And how are you this morning,
And is it time to play?"
"BAAA, BAAA,"
That's how they say "Good day".
"BAAA, BAAA,"
That's how they say "Good day".

When dogs get up in the morning,
They always say, "Good day,
And how are you this morning,
And is it time to play?"
"BOWW, WOWW,"
That's how they say "Good day".
"BOWW, WOWW,"
That's how they say "Good day".

When cats get up in the morning,
They always say, "Good day,
And how are you this morning,
And is it time to play?"
"MEOW, MEOW,"
That's how they say "Good day".
"MEOW, MEOW,"
That's how they say "Good day".

JUST FOR FUN

HEY DIDDLE DIDDLE

Hey diddle diddle,
The cat and the fiddle,
The cow jumped over the moon.
The little dog laughed
To see such fun,
And the dish ran away with the spoon.

DIDDLETY, DIDDLETY, DUMPTY

Diddlety, diddlety, dumpty,
The cat ran up the plum tree.
Half-a-crown
To fetch her down,
Diddlety, diddlety, dumpty.

PAT-A-CAKE, PAT-A-CAKE

Pat-a-cake, pat-a-cake, baker's man,
Bake me a cake as fast as you can.
Pat it and prick it and mark it with B
And put in the oven for Baby and me.

HICKORY, DICKORY, DOCK

Hickory, dickory, dock,
The mouse ran up the clock.
The clock struck one,
The mouse ran down,
Hickory, dickory, dock.

TO MARKET, TO MARKET

To market, to market, to buy a fat pig,
Home again, home again, jiggety-jig.
To market, to market to buy a fat hog,
Home again, home again, jiggety-jog.

MR FROG

Mr Frog, he jumped out of the pond one day
And he found himself in the rain.
Said he, "I'll get wet and I might catch a cold,"
So he jumped in the pond again.

DANCE TO YOUR DADDY

Dance to your daddy,
My little babby,
Dance to your daddy,
My little lamb.

You shall have a fishy
In a little dishy,
You shall have a fishy
When the boat comes in.

THIS IS THE WAY THE LADIES RIDE

This is the way the ladies ride,
Trippety-trot,
Trippety-trot.
This is the way the ladies ride,
Trippety trippety-trot.

This is the way the gentlemen ride,
Gallop-a-lop,
Gallop-a-lop.
This is the way the gentlemen ride,
Gallop-a-gallop-a-lop.

This is the way the farmers ride,
Hobbledy-hoy,
Hobbledy-hoy.
This is the way the farmers ride,
Hobbledy hobbledy-hoy.

RIDE A COCK-HORSE

Ride a cock-horse to Banbury Cross,
To see a fine lady upon a white horse;
With rings on her fingers and bells on her toes,
She shall have music wherever she goes.

RING-A-RING O' ROSES

Ring-a-ring o' roses,
A pocket full of posies,
Atishoo! Atishoo!
We all fall down.

ROUND AND ROUND
THE GARDEN

Round and round the garden
Like a teddy bear,
One step, two step,
And tickly under there.

How Curious

There Was a Crooked Man

There was a crooked man, and he went a crooked mile,
He found a crooked sixpence against a crooked stile.
He bought a crooked cat, which caught a crooked mouse,
And they all lived together in a little crooked house.

SIMPLE SIMON

Simple Simon met a pieman,
Going to the fair;
Said Simple Simon to the pieman,
"Let me taste your ware."

Said the pieman then to Simon,
"Show me first your penny."
Said Simple Simon to the pieman,
"Sir, I have not any."

I Went to the Animal Fair

I went to the animal fair,
The birds and the beasts were there,
The big baboon by the light of the moon
Was combing his auburn hair.
The monkey fell out of his bunk,
And slid down the elephant's trunk,
The elephant sneezed and fell on his knees,
But what became of the monkey, monkey, monk...

THERE WAS AN OLD WOMAN

There was an old woman who lived in a shoe.
She had so many children, she didn't know what to do.
She gave them some broth without any bread,
She kissed them all gently and put them to bed.

OLD MOTHER HUBBARD

Old Mother Hubbard
Went to the cupboard
To get her poor dog a bone,
But when she came there
The cupboard was bare,
And so the poor dog had none.

THE GRAND OLD DUKE OF YORK

O, the grand old Duke of York,
He had ten thousand men,
He marched them up to the top of the hill
And he marched them down again!

And when they were up they were up,
And when they were down they were down,
And when they were only halfway up
They were neither up nor down.

48

O, the grand old Duke of York
Had woollen underpants,
He wore them on some cold campaigns
In the battlefields of France.

And when they were up they were up,
And when they were down they were down,
And when they were only halfway up
He wore a puzzled frown.

Rub a Dub Dub

Rub a dub dub
Three men in a tub,
And who do you think they be?
The butcher, the baker,
The candlestick maker,
And they set out to sea.

Jack Sprat

Jack Sprat could eat no fat,
His wife could eat no lean,
And so between the both of them
They licked the platter clean.

HUMPTY DUMPTY

Humpty Dumpty sat on a wall,
Humpty Dumpty had a great fall.
All the king's horses and all the king's men
Couldn't put Humpty together again.

THE QUEEN OF HEARTS

The Queen of Hearts,
She made some tarts,
All on a summer's day.
The Knave of Hearts,
He stole those tarts,
And took them clean away.

The King of Hearts
Called for the tarts,
And beat the Knave full sore.
The Knave of Hearts
Brought back the tarts,
And vowed he'd steal no more.

MARY, MARY, QUITE CONTRARY

Mary, Mary, quite contrary,
How does your garden grow?
With silver bells and cockle shells,
And pretty maids all in a row.

There Was a Little Girl

There was a little girl who had a little curl
Right in the middle of her forehead.
When she was good, she was very, very good
But when she was bad, she was horrid.

I Had a Little Nut Tree

I had a little nut tree, nothing would it bear
But a silver nutmeg and a golden pear.
The King of Spain's daughter came to visit me,
And all for the sake of my little nut tree.

SING A SONG OF SIXPENCE

Sing a song of sixpence,
A pocket full of rye,
Four and twenty blackbirds
Baked in a pie.

When the pie was opened,
The birds began to sing;
Was not that a dainty dish
To set before a king?

The king was in his counting house
Counting out his money;
The queen was in the parlour,
Eating bread and honey;

The maid was in the garden,
Hanging out the clothes,
When down flew a blackbird,
And pecked off her nose.

She made such a commotion
That little Jenny Wren
Flew down into the garden
And popped it on again.

OUTDOORS

WHO HAS SEEN THE WIND

Who has seen the wind?
Neither I nor you:
But when the leaves hang trembling
The wind is passing through.

Who has seen the wind?
Neither you nor I:
But when the trees bow down their heads
The wind is passing by.

RED SKY AT NIGHT

Red sky at night, shepherd's delight;
Red sky in the morning, shepherd's warning.

IT'S RAINING, IT'S POURING

It's raining, it's pouring,
The old man is snoring,
He went to bed and bumped his head
And couldn't get up in the morning.

Rain, Rain, Go Away

Rain, rain, go away,
Come back another day.

A Sunshiny Shower

A sunshiny shower
Won't last half an hour.

Rain at Seven

Rain at seven,
Fine by eleven.

A rainbow afternoon,
Good weather coming soon.

THE NORTH WIND DOTH BLOW

The north wind doth blow,
And we shall have snow,
And what will the robin do then,
Poor thing?
He'll sit in the barn
And keep himself warm
And hide his head under his wing,
Poor thing!

The north wind doth blow
And we shall have snow,
And what will the dormouse do then,
Poor thing?
Rolled up like a ball
In his nest snug and small,
He'll sleep till warm weather comes in,
Poor thing!

BOATS SAIL ON THE RIVERS

Boats sail on the rivers,
And ships sail on the seas;
But clouds that sail across the sky
Are prettier far than these.

There are bridges on the rivers,
As pretty as you please;
But the bow that bridges heaven,
And overtops the trees,
And builds a road from earth to sky,
Is prettier far than these.

O DANDELION

"O dandelion, yellow as gold,
What do you do all day?"

"I just wait here in the tall green grass
Till the children come to play."

"O dandelion, yellow as gold,
What do you do all night?"

"I wait and wait till the cool dews fall
And my hair grows long and white."

"And what do you do when your hair is white
And the children come to play?"

"They take me up in their dimpled hands
And blow my hair away!"

Great Oaks from Little Acorns Grow

Great oaks from little acorns grow
And grow and grow
So tall and slow.

From great oaks little acorns grow
They fall below
And grow and grow.

OVER IN THE MEADOW

Over in the meadow
By a pond in the sun
Lived an old mother duckie
And her little duckie one.
"Quack," said the mother,
"Quack, quack," said the one.
And they quacked and were happy
By the pond in the sun.

Over in the meadow
Where the stream runs blue
Lived an old mother fish
And her baby fishes two.
"Swim," said the mother,
"We swim," said the two,
And they swam and were happy
Where the stream runs blue.

Over in the meadow
In a nest in a tree
Lived an old mother sparrow
And her hatchlings three.
"Sing," said the mother,
"We sing," said the three,
And they sang and were happy
In their nest in a tree.

Over in the meadow
On the mud by the shore
Lived an old mother frog
And her little froggies four.
"Hop," said the mother,
"We hop," said the four,
And they hopped and were happy
On the mud by the shore.

Over in the meadow
In a straw beehive
Lived an old mother queen bee
And her honeybees five.
"Hum," said the queen,
"Hmmm, hmmm," said the five,
And they hummed and were happy
In their straw beehive.

Over in the meadow
In the evening sun
Danced a pretty mother
And her baby one.
"Look," said the mother,
"At the ducks and the bees,
At the frogs and the fish
And the birds in the trees."

"We hum," said the five,
"We hop," said the four,
"We sing," said the three,
"We swim," said the two,
"Quack, quack," said the one,
And they all played together
Till the day was done.

COUNTING

HOW MANY DAYS HAS MY BABY TO PLAY?

How many days has my baby to play?
Saturday, Sunday, Monday,
Tuesday, Wednesday, Thursday, Friday,
Saturday, Sunday, Monday.

TWO LITTLE DICKY BIRDS

Two little dicky birds
Sat upon a wall,
One named Peter,
The other named Paul.

Fly away Peter!
Fly away Paul!
Come back Peter,
Come back Paul.

FIVE LITTLE DUCKS

Five little ducks went out one day
Over the hills and far away.
Mother duck said, "Quack, quack, quack, quack."
But only four little ducks came back.

Four little ducks went out one day
Over the hills and far away.
Mother duck said, "Quack, quack, quack, quack."
But only three little ducks came back.

Three little ducks went out one day
Over the hills and far away.
Mother duck said, "Quack, quack, quack, quack."
But only two little ducks came back.

Two little ducks went out one day
Over the hills and far away.
Mother duck said, "Quack, quack, quack, quack."
But only one little duck came back.

THIS LITTLE PIGGY

This little piggy went to market,

This little piggy stayed home,

This little piggy had roast beef,

This little piggy had none,

And this little piggy went wee, wee, wee
All the way home.

ONE, TWO, THREE, FOUR, FIVE

1, 2, 3, 4, 5
Once I caught a fish alive
6, 7, 8, 9, 10
Then I let him go again.
Why did you let him go?
Because he bit my finger so.
Which finger did he bite?
This little finger on the right.

FIVE GREEN AND SPECKLED FROGS

Five green and speckled frogs
Sat on a speckled log
Eating some most delicious bugs:
YUM YUM.
One jumped into a pool
Where it was nice and cool
Then there were four green speckled frogs.

Four green and speckled frogs
Sat on a speckled log
Eating some most delicious bugs:
YUM YUM.
One jumped into a pool
Where it was nice and cool
Then there were three green speckled frogs.

Three green and speckled frogs
Sat on a speckled log
Eating some most delicious bugs:
YUM YUM.
One jumped into a pool
Where it was nice and cool
Then there were two green speckled frogs.

Two green and speckled frogs
Sat on a speckled log
Eating some most delicious bugs:
YUM YUM.
One jumped into a pool
Where it was nice and cool
Then there was one green speckled frog.

One green and speckled frog
Sat on a speckled log
Eating some most delicious bugs:
YUM YUM.
She jumped into a pool
Where it was nice and cool
Then there were no green speckled frogs.

THREE LITTLE MEN IN A FLYING SAUCER

Three little men in a flying saucer
Came down to earth one day.
They looked left and right
But they didn't like the sight
So one man flew away.

Two little men in a flying saucer
Came down to earth one day.
They looked left and right
But they didn't like the sight
So one man flew away.

One little man in a flying saucer
Came down to earth one day.
He looked left and right
But he didn't like the sight
So he upped and flew away.

ONE, TWO, BUCKLE MY SHOE

One, two, buckle my shoe

Three, four, knock at the door

Five, six, pick up sticks
Seven, eight, lay them straight

Nine, ten, a big fat hen

Eleven, twelve, dig and delve

Thirteen, fourteen, maids
a-courting

Fifteen, sixteen, maids in
the kitchen

Seventeen, eighteen, maids
in waiting

Nineteen, twenty,
my plate's empty.

GOODNIGHT

WEE WILLIE WINKIE

Wee Willie Winkie
Runs through the town,
Upstairs and downstairs
In his nightgown,
Rapping at the window,
Crying through the lock,
"Are the children in their beds?
For now it's eight o'clock."

THE MAN IN THE MOON

The man in the moon
Looked out of the moon
And this is what he said:
" 'Tis time that, now I'm getting up,
All babies went to bed."

DIDDLE, DIDDLE, DUMPLING

Diddle, diddle, dumpling, my son John,
Went to bed with his trousers on.
One shoe off, and one shoe on,
Diddle, diddle, dumpling, my son John.

All Day Long

All day long
The sun shines bright.
The moon and stars
Come out by night.
From twilight time
They line the skies
And watch the world
With quiet eyes.

I SEE THE MOON

I see the moon
And the moon sees me;
God bless the moon
And God bless me.

Climb a Silver Ladder

Climb a silver ladder
To the moon above.
Pick a bowl of starlight
For the one you love.

Twinkle, Twinkle, Little Star

Twinkle, twinkle, little star,
How I wonder what you are!
Up above the world so high,
Like a diamond in the sky.

STAR LIGHT, STAR BRIGHT

Star light, star bright,
First star I see tonight,
I wish I may, I wish I might,
Have the wish I wish tonight.

GO TO SLEEP, MY DARLING

Go to sleep, my darling,
Close your pretty eyes.
Angels up above you
Peep down from the skies.

HUSH-A-BYE, BABY

Hush-a-bye, baby, on the tree top!
When the wind blows the cradle will rock
When the bough breaks the cradle will fall
Down will come baby, cradle and all.

COME TO THE WINDOW

Come to the window,
My baby, with me,
And look at the stars
That shine on the sea!
There are two little stars
That play bo-peep
With two little fish
Far down in the deep;
And two little frogs
Cry, "Neap, neap, neap;"
I see a dear baby
Who should be asleep.

Hush, Little Baby

Hush, little baby, don't say a word,
Mama's going to buy you a mockingbird.

And if that mockingbird don't sing,
Mama's going to buy you a diamond ring.

And if that diamond ring turns brass,
Mama's going to buy you a looking glass.

And if that looking glass gets broke,
Mama's going to buy you a billy goat.

And if that billy goat won't pull,
Mama's going to buy you a cart and bull.

And if that cart and bull turn over,
Mama's going to buy you a dog named Rover.

And if that dog named Rover won't bark,
Mama's going to buy you a horse and cart.

And if that horse and cart fall down,
You'll still be the sweetest little baby in town.

THE MOON SHINES BRIGHT

The moon shines bright,
The stars give light
Before the break of day;
God bless you all
Both great and small
And send a joyful day.

A Candle, a Candle

A candle, a candle to light me to bed,
A pillow, a pillow to prop up your head,
A quilt made of patches to tuck you up tight,
A hug and a kiss and a very good night.

INDEX OF FIRST LINES